THE

WITCH'S

HANDBOOK

D1431628

THE

WITCH'S

HANDBOOK

by Rachel Dickinson

PSS!
PRICE STERN SLOAN

www.quirkproductions.com

Designed by Paul Kepple and Timothy Crawford @ Headcase Design
Layout by Hotfoot Studio

Published by Price Stern Sloan, a division of Penguin Putnam Books for Young Readers, 345 Hudson Street, New York, NY 10014.

PSS! is a registered trademark of Penguin Putnam Inc.

Printed in Singapore.

Library of Congress Control Number: 2002104248

ISBN: 0-8431-4917-5

A B C D E F G H I J

PHOTOGRAPHY CREDITS

pg. ii: Photofest

pg. vi: Photofest

pg. 3: Photofest

pg. 7: Photofest

pg. 11: Photofest

pg. 12: Photofest

pg. 13: Photofest

pg. 14: Photofest

pg. 15: Walt Disney Productions

pg. 16: Photofest

pg. 17: Photofest

pg. 18: Photofest

pg. 21: Photofest

pg. 26: Paul and Lindamarie Ambrose/Getty

pg. 32: Photofest

pg. 35: Photofest

pg. 38: Photofest

pgs. 50–51: Photofest

pg. 53: Photofest

pg. 54: Photofest

pg. 56: Photofest

pg. 82: Photofest

CONTENTS

DID I LEAVE MY CAULDRON BOILING?

TODAY'S FASHIONABLE WITCH WEARS A HAT THAT SUITS HIS OR HER STYLE—OR GOES BAREHEADED.

ARE YOU A WITCH?

When most people imagine a witch, they think of a nasty old hag with long stringy hair, a tall pointy black hat, and a wart on the end of her nose. There may be a broom, a black cat, and a bubbling cauldron nearby. She might be cackling evilly or cooking up a nasty potion by stirring eye of newt and dragon's liver into her simmering cauldron.

This is the kind of witch that fairy tales usually describe, and that movies and television often portray. But this isn't the whole story. The truth is, a witch can be a regular person—male or female, nice or nasty—who has a feel for magic.

Have you ever wondered if you had magical potential? Have you ever felt like you knew what was going to happen before it happened? That could be a kind of magic called divination, or future-seeing. Do you find that you have an especially friendly relationship with cats—particularly black ones? Instead of shrieking and running away when you come across a spider or a toad, do you want to go get a closer look? That could be a special ability to communicate with magical animals. Do you feel very energetic whenever there's a full moon? That could be a magical ability to focus energy. Are you attracted to pointy hats? *Hmmm.*

Maybe you're really a witch but haven't developed your powers yet.

Witches have been around for centuries but have had a rotten reputation until the last couple of decades. Today, witches look just like everyone else. No more warty noses. Gone are the bad hair days. Anyone who feels like they have a little magic inside them or is interested in spells and charms can learn to let the witch inside come out.

YOU CAN LET YOUR INNER WITCH COME OUT!

THE WITCH INSIDE YOU

Look around you. Your school librarian could be a witch. Or your gym teacher. Or even your mom. If you really think you or someone you know might be a witch—take the following exam to rate witching potential:

FEDERAL WITCH IDENTIFICATION EXAM
3033 EZ

❶	**Are you fond of black pointy hats?**
◯	**A.** Yes
☑	**B.** No
◯	**C.** I'm afraid of getting hat hair.

❷	**Do you have a particular fondness for cats, toads, or owls?**
◯	**A.** Yes
☑	**B.** Sort of, but I'm a bit grossed out by the toads.
◯	**C.** No, I like dogs and horses.

3 If you have a stick or straw in your hand, do you find yourself waving it around—almost like a wand?

- ✓ **A.** Sometimes
- ○ **B.** Yes, and sometimes I think I feel vibrations.
- ○ **C.** I don't like to pick up sticks, it's too much like yard work.

4 Do you find yourself speaking in rhymes?

- ○ **A.** Yes
- ○ **B.** Only when I'm trying to annoy my mom.
- ✓ **C.** Why would anyone do that?

5 Do you feel particularly happy during full moons?

- ○ **A.** Yes
- ○ **B.** I'm not quite sure when a full moon happens.
- ○ **C.** The moon changes shape?

6 Do you find yourself often helping your friends find lost objects?

- ✓ **A.** Yes, sometimes I just know where they are.
- ○ **B.** No, never.
- ○ **C.** I like to help but I'm not very good at finding things.

7 **Do you sometimes sneeze or wink and suddenly things . . . happen?**

○ **A.** Yes, does this happen to others as well?

✓ **B.** Things happen all the time, no matter what I do—what kind of things are we talking about?

○ **C.** It's just a nervous twitch.

8 **Have you ever wanted a broomstick of your very own?**

✓ **A.** Of course, I see nice ones all the time.

○ **B.** I think my mom has a broom in the closet.

○ **C.** What's a broomstick?

Add up your points:

1 a) 3 b) 1 c) 2
2 a) 3 b) 2 c) 1
3 a) 2 b) 3 c) 1
4 a) 3 b) 2 c) 1
5 a) 3 b) 2 c) 1
6 a) 3 b) 1 c) 2
7 a) 3 b) 1 c) 2
8 a) 3 b) 2 c) 1

YOUR SCORE:

8–12 points
Some witching potential—it may increase with practice

13–18 points
Very strong witching potential

19–24 points
Yes! There is a witch here!

① + ② = HAPPY DURING FULL MOON ③ FONDNESS FOR CATS

No matter how you scored on the Federal Witch Identification Exam, keep reading because you wouldn't have picked up this book if you didn't have some affinity for witches, witchcraft, and all things witchy. Take some time to write down the reasons why you think you—or someone you know —might be a witch. This will be good practice because if you decide to develop your witching potential, you'll soon be making these same kinds of notes in your own private witch's journal (see pp. 88–89). For example, write down any dreams you've had in which magical things occurred. Or if you've made any wishes that have come true. Or if you've had an irresistible urge to wear a long, black cloak.

SEVEN REASONS I THINK I MIGHT BE A WITCH:

1

2

3

4

5

6

7

Throughout history there have been lovable witches as well as not-so-nice ones. It all depends on how they behaved.

LITTLE WITCH

In these books, which you may have read when you were younger, Little Witch gets in trouble because she makes the mistake of being *too* good—she makes her bed and cleans the cobwebs out of her closet, but in her world, witches are supposed to cause mischief. One time, when Little Witch has been behaving much too well, her mother and aunts punish her by flying out without her on Halloween, leaving Little Witch to hold down the spooky mansion by herself. She ends up giving rides on her broomstick to trick-or-treaters who dare to come to the mansion. Little Witch's relatives look like traditional scary witches in black dresses with pointy hats on top of messy hair, but Little Witch asserts her independence by wearing a black dress over a red-and-white striped shirt and tights, and a red ribbon tied around her hat.

KIKI

In the animated movie *Kiki's Delivery Service*, when Kiki turns 13 she leaves home to discover her own special talents. She and her black cat, Jiji, set up a flying delivery service for a nearby bakery, and it becomes a rousing success. In this coming-of-age story Kiki learns that a good witch must have confidence in herself to be able to perform good magic. (Kiki was created by the famous Japanese anime artist, Hayao Miyazaki. Yes, they have witches in Japan, too!)

GLINDA

One of the most famous of the good witches, Glinda makes her first appearance in *The Wizard of Oz* as a giant bubble that floats out of the sky. Glinda actually looks more like a princess than a witch, with a sparkly pink gown and a crown (she may have been trying to disguise herself)—though she does carry a wand. Glinda also has a silvery-sounding voice; her first question to Dorothy is, "Are you a good witch or a bad witch?" because Dorothy's house has just swirled out of the sky into Oz, which would lead anyone to wonder what kind of witch she was. Glinda's magic tends to be less spectacular than that of her relative, the Wicked Witch of the West (see "Witches We Love to Hate"), but she has the power of goodness behind her.

SAMANTHA STEVENS

Samantha Stevens was one of the first of the modern witches (the kind who look just like everyone else) to be portrayed on TV, in the 1960s sitcom *Bewitched*. Samantha and her husband,

Darrin, live in the suburbs, where Samantha tries to blend in with the neighboring mortals. Instead of using a wand, Samantha wrinkles up and twitches her nose (like a rabbit does when it's looking for food) when she does magic. Because Darrin is a mortal and wants to live a "normal" life, he doesn't want Samantha using her magic—to the dismay of the rest of her weird, witchy family. But she's a witch after all—why dust and sweep when a simple twitch of the nose cleans the whole house and gets dinner on the table?

The witches who show up in fairy tales tend to be truly rotten witches. They may be disguised as old hags or beautiful queens, but boy, do they cause trouble. How many of these can you recognize?

CHILD-EATING WITCH

You may recall this one! When Hansel and Gretel are sent into the forest by their father and wicked stepmother they stumble upon a delicious house made of gingerbread and decorated with candy and cookies. That should have been their first clue that something wasn't quite right. It turns out the witch who lives inside actually likes to eat children—and she shuts Hansel and Gretel up in cages and feeds them a lot to fatten them up. Fortunately, it's the witch who ends up cooked, not the kids!

MALEFICENT

The witch in the story of Sleeping Beauty is one of the creepiest sorceresses to be found in fairy tales. Maleficent casts a spell on a baby and then waits 18 years to lure the girl into a castle room to give her spinning lessons to complete the spell. We all know not to talk to strangers but Sleeping Beauty was raised in the forest and never had much contact with the outside world. Maleficent is very powerful and can conjure up impenetrable thorny forests and scary creatures. She can also change her shape and turn into a dragon. But like all bad witches in good fairy tales, her evil plans are foiled in the end.

WICKED WITCH OF THE WEST

Now this is one scary witch—but she's kind of cool, too. In addition to sporting traditional garb—pointy black hat and a long flowing black dress—she has the longest, crooked-est, most warty nose in witch history. And she's green. Probably the most menacing thing about her is her cackling, wicked laugh. Listen to her threaten Dorothy: "I'm going to get you my pretty, and your little dog too!" You get a chill down your spine no matter how many times you've seen *The Wizard of Oz*! But, boy, can that gal ever ride a broomstick—check out the skywriting she does above Emerald City. Not to mention those flying monkey sidekicks.

CONVENTION OF WITCHES

Roald Dahl's book *The Witches* (and the movie of the same name) reveals a bunch of witches who meet at an annual convention in an English seaside hotel—under the name of "Royal Society for the Prevention of Cruelty to Children." The irony is that these witches despise children—kids smell like dog droppings to their sensitive noses—so the witches are plotting to turn the children of England into mice. These witches are particularly ugly. To blend into the mortal population they have to wear masks, wigs, and gloves to cover up their hideous faces, bald heads, and scaly hands with long, pointy fingernails.

SCHOOLS FOR WITCHING

Even witches have to go to school, and the most famous school for learning the fine art of witchery is found in the Harry Potter series by J. K. Rowling—it's Hogwarts School of Witchcraft and Wizardry. Subjects include Transfiguration, Casting Spells, Divination, and Defense against the Dark Arts. The problem with Hogwarts is there are no application forms anywhere, so no one can apply to get in. The admissions committee knows which kids have witch talent, and decides who should attend the school— then sends students an invitation by way of an owl.

THE FACULTY AT HOGWARTS ARE ALL PRACTICING WIZARDS AND WITCHES.

HOW TO RECOGNIZE A FELLOW WITCH

Witches, especially young witches, look a lot like other people—but there are certain telltale signs that can help you recognize them.

Pointy hat: Even the most modern witch probably has one somewhere, and traditional witches simply won't go out without one. A witch who's trying to blend in might try to disguise the hat. Watch out for a knitted stocking cap that sticks straight up, for example, or someone wearing a dunce cap—it's probably really a witch's hat.

Brooms: Since a lot of witches use them for transportation, they generally keep one within reach. Be suspicious of anyone who sweeps wherever they go—on the street, at other people's homes, in school—this type of witch may be hiding in plain sight.

Cat or other companion animal: A witch's coworker in animal form, often called a familiar, is likely to be nearby. Be alert for anyone who is regularly accompanied by the same animal—if you hear the two of them whispering, it's for sure you've seen a witch!

GOOD WITCH OR BAD WITCH? HOW TO TELL

Remember when Glinda asks Dorothy in *The Wizard of Oz*, "Are you a good witch or a bad witch?" Instead of asking straight out, there are a few things you can look for.

- **Good Witch:** Smiles a lot, revealing white teeth; has a musical laugh; smells nice; has clean hair; wears colorful clothing; is helpful; enjoys sunshine as well as moonlight; has a garden full of colorful flowers and good-smelling herbs; has a friendly familiar.

• **Bad Witch:** Evil grin with discolored teeth; cackles instead of laughs; might wear gloves to hide scaly hands and pointy fingernails; every day is a bad hair day; may smell like rotten eggs (especially when working evil spells); prefers all black clothing; has a garden full of moldy plants and toadstools; has a nasty familiar.

GOOD VS. BAD, WHICH WITCH IS WHICH?

① ESSENTIALS | ② HAIR & MAKEUP | ③ MANICURE | ④ APPAREL

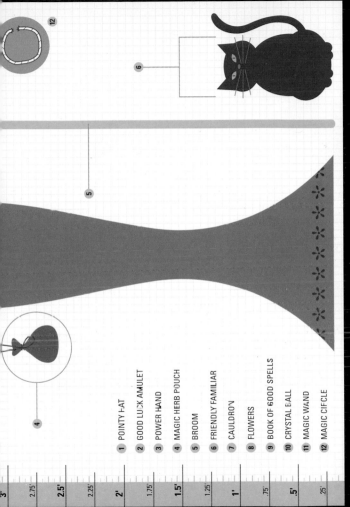

1. POINTY HAT
2. GOOD LUCK AMULET
3. POWER HAND
4. MAGIC HERB POUCH
5. BROOM
6. FRIENDLY FAMILIAR
7. CAULDRON
8. FLOWERS
9. BOOK OF GOOD SPELLS
10. CRYSTAL BALL
11. MAGIC WAND
12. MAGIC CIRCLE

GOOD WITCH CHARACTERISTICS: THEY ARE KIND, SMELL NICE, AND CAST GOOD SPELLS.

3'
2.75"
2.5'
2.25"
2'
1.75"
1.5'
1.25"
1'
.75'
.5'
.25"

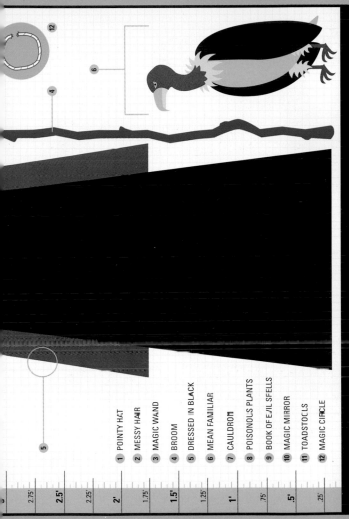

1. POINTY HAT
2. MESSY HAIR
3. MAGIC WAND
4. BROOM
5. DRESSED IN BLACK
6. MEAN FAMILIAR
7. CAULDRON
8. POISONOUS PLANTS
9. BOOK OF EVIL SPELLS
10. MAGIC MIRROR
11. TOADSTOOLS
12. MAGIC CIRCLE

BAD WITCH CHARACTERISTICS: THEY ARE MEAN, SMELL BAD, AND CAST SPELLS FOR EVIL.

CHAPTER TWO

WITCHERY IN HISTORY

For many, many years, witches were terribly misunderstood. If they used their magic openly—say in trying to save a village from a rampaging dragon—they were in danger of being hauled into court by professional witch-hunters (particularly if the witch couldn't stop the dragon, who then ate a few villagers!). This forced many witches into hiding. They'd meet at night in the middle of the woods to discuss the latest potions and spells—this way they could continue to do their witchy business and keep it hidden from snooping, suspicious people who didn't understand magic.

Some really ignorant people thought they would be happier if they got rid of everything they couldn't understand. (This attitude is what drove the dragons into deep hiding in caves and the unicorns into the middle of the deepest, darkest forests.) This wrong-headed thinking led some people to try to capture witches and burn them at the stake—but rest assured, captured witches simply cast anti-burning protection spells on themselves and disappeared. Fortunately, all of this silliness stopped a couple of hundred years ago.

WITCH KNOWLEDGE THROUGH THE AGES

Throughout history, in addition to the basic principles of magic, witches have learned a lot about nature and the earth, and especially how plants—their roots, leaves, and even bark—could heal wounds and cure illness. A lot of people thought this plant knowledge was magic. Well, the truth is, some of it is and some of it isn't—only today's witches know for sure!

If you had lived before the days of Band-Aids and anti-bacterial ointment, you'd have wanted to know some plant magic too! In their travels through the countryside, witches noticed and gathered bits and pieces of all the various plants that grew (even from the tops of trees because, after all, they were on their broomsticks). They picked leaves, berries, stems, and flowers to stir into potions. Eventually they figured out which plants and herbs could help cure people who were sick and which ones might actually harm them. Many of today's modern drugs are created from plants once used by witches and other healers.

Imagine the responsibility of healing every person who fell down and scraped his or her knee, or got burned by hot dragon's breath, or came down with a bad ear infection. Sometimes things didn't go as planned and a patient might get worse rather than better. In those cases, the entire village might blame a witch who was only doing his or her best to help. That's why witches to this day are very careful not to let just anyone know about their powers.

MAGICAL PLANTS

Plants are quite versatile—they have medicinal and magical properties, and witches use them in all sorts of ways—they may boil plants up in water to make magic tea, grind them into flakes for use in potions, or occasionally take a charmed bath with them! Here are some of the most useful types of plants:

TO BREAK CURSES: ○	PEPPER, MISTLETOE
FOR HAPPINESS: ○	ALLSPICE, SANDALWOOD
TO BANISH NIGHTMARES: ○	ANISE, HYACINTH, MORNING GLORY
TO STOP GOSSIP: ○	CLOVES
TO ATTRACT LOVE: ○	APPLE, ORANGE BLOSSOMS
FOR PEACE: ○	HUCKLEBERRY ROOT, VANILLA
FOR PROTECTION: ○	BASIL, GARLIC, PEPPER
FOR WEALTH: ○	DILL SEED, PINE NEEDLES, TURNIP

THE MODERN WITCH

Today's witches look like everyone else. They wear ordinary clothing and have ordinary jobs. Some witches like to get together for parties and celebrate special witch holidays—like Samhain and Imbolc (see the Witch Holidays on p. 36)—and to do some good magic together. What's neat about

MODERN WITCHES OFTEN GET TOGETHER TO DISCUSS MUNDANE THINGS LIKE THE RISING COST OF FLYING BROOM MAINTENANCE.

being a witch is that you can be a witch alone or with other people—it's up to the witch. Some people think "the more the merrier" when it comes to doing something new, while others prefer to work alone. Consider inviting your friends over to try and create some new and nifty spells.

EVERYDAY MAGIC

Even though you don't often see a dragon lurking about or even a witch flying by on a broomstick these days, it doesn't mean that there isn't any magic in the world. It's just more subtle than that. Look around you. How many times have you heard someone say something like, "What an amazing coincidence!" when something happens that seems remarkable and can't quite be explained. Is there really any such thing as a coincidence? Or is it really . . . magic?

A WITCH'S CALENDAR

Many modern witches call their annual calendar the "Wheel of the Year" to highlight the idea that the seasons are part of an ongoing and never-ending cycle. The wheel is divided into eight parts (think of a wheel with spokes) with a sabbat, or holiday, at the beginning of each cycle of the wheel. These occasions are not unlike our holidays, when we sit around with family and friends, and eat too much food. Witches' holidays also involve feasting. All the witches bring a dish to share—like sautéed dragon's liver and spinach tossed with an essence of powdered toad dressing.

Witch holidays are also good days for doing magic. Spells created during the Witch holidays or on full moons are more powerful than those created at other times.

WOULD YOU LIKE TO SHARE A MEAL OF LIZARD AND TOADSTOOL STEW, SERVED IN A JACK-O'-LANTERN BOWL?

WITCH HOLIDAYS

SAMHAIN (SOW-een), known to non-witches as Halloween (October 31), is the Witch New Year, and like everyone else, witches like to have a party. It's a good time for witches to get together because all the non-witches are dressed in costume and the real witches can blend right in!

YULE (YOOL) or Winter Solstice (December 21) is the longest night of the year, making it a good time for spells that require the cover of darkness.

IMBOLC (IM-bulk), known to non-witches as Groundhog Day (February 2), marks the halfway point between Winter Solstice and Spring Equinox. The days are getting longer and spring is on its way, which is reassuring for witches who live in colder climates and are tired of trying to create magic circles in the snow.

OSTARA (Oh-STAR-uh) or Spring Equinox (March 21) is when day and night are equal in length—time to start exploring outdoors in search of good stones for your stone magic (see Chapter 4). If you feel your wand is losing power, it's also a good time to look for a straight, strong stick for a new wand.

BELTANE (BEL-tain) or May Day (May 1) is time to welcome the spring. They did this in the olden days by dancing around a Maypole. You could probably just go outside and enjoy the nice weather.

MIDSUMMER or Summer Solstice (June 21) is the longest day of the year. Traditionally, witches have a feast on this day. You could have a picnic lunch with friends.

LAMMAS or First Harvest (August 1) was traditionally the time when the first crops were harvested. Witches can celebrate by eating some fresh vegetables. Or maybe not.

MABON (MAY-bahn) or Autumn Equinox (September 21) is when day and night are again equal. It's also the beginning of the school year, so young witches everywhere will be looking over their new classmates, wondering, "good witch or a bad witch?"

FLOWERS

NOTEBOOK

STONES

HERBS

POT

TWIGS

STRING

CHAPTER THREE

WITCH ESSENTIALS

Every witch needs a few basic things for practicing magic. Think of it as a witch's toolkit.

BROOMSTICK

Witches and broomsticks go together like peanut butter and jelly. Broomsticks have long been associated with magic. In olden times, people would place one across the doorstep to ward off evil spirits or under the pillow to protect them while they slept and give them pleasant dreams. (They'd have had to pile up a couple of pillows so as not to keep waking up because of the hard piece of wood under their head.) A witch's broomstick was also called a "besom" (BEE-sum). It takes a special kind of broomstick to serve a witch or wizard's purposes. For example, the broomsticks that Harry Potter and his friends use—the Nimbus 2000 or the Firebolt—can definitely take a person for a ride.

WITCH'S JOURNAL

Your Witch's Journal is where you keep track of your magical experiences. You should also write down all of your spells and note when you have used them and whether or not they worked.

① **Start with a blank book**—you can even use a spiral notebook—and write "My Witch's Journal" on the first page with your name and the date. You might want to decorate the cover with cut-outs or drawings. Then every time you encounter anything magical, jot it down. There's an example on page 88 of one way to organize your journal.

② **Note any unusual weather**, such as a very loud thunderstorm or a rain of toads.

③ **Keep track of the full moons** (remember that magic is at its strongest during the full moon and on the major witch holidays).

④ **Write in your best cursive handwriting**, and use different colored ink pens (read about the magical properties associated with colors on p. 70).

Remember, this is your own Witch's Journal with your impressions, observations, and spells in it. However, if you want to start a witches' group, you can create a journal for the whole gang.

MAKE YOUR OWN BROOMSTICK

Witches' broomsticks aren't necessarily like the ones found in your kitchen at home. For one thing, they don't have to be able to sweep anything up because they're used primarily as a means of transportation.

SUPPLIES

○ Twigs

○ A long straight dowel (a mop handle works nicely)

○ String or cord (about one yard or meter in length)

○ Tape (masking tape or duct tape will do)

1. Go out into your backyard or a wooded area and gather about 20 or 30 twigs. At certain times of the year, or after a big storm, you should be able to find these lying on the ground underneath big trees. Your twigs should be fairly straight and at least a foot (30 cm) long.

   Try to avoid brittle sticks because they'll just break when you try to work with them.

2

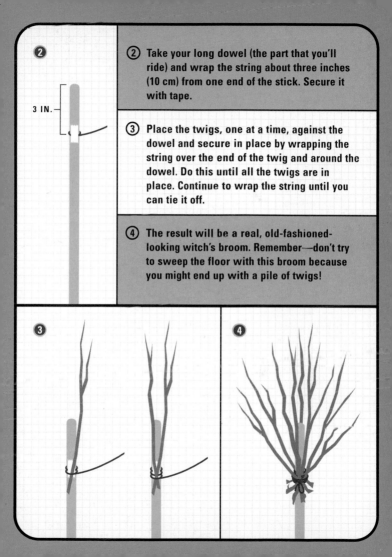

3 IN.

2. Take your long dowel (the part that you'll ride) and wrap the string about three inches (10 cm) from one end of the stick. Secure it with tape.

3. Place the twigs, one at a time, against the dowel and secure in place by wrapping the string over the end of the twig and around the dowel. Do this until all the twigs are in place. Continue to wrap the string until you can tie it off.

4. The result will be a real, old-fashioned-looking witch's broom. Remember—don't try to sweep the floor with this broom because you might end up with a pile of twigs!

3

4

THE CIRCLE

Witches perform most of their magic within a magic circle. A magic circle is one that becomes a place of power and energy created by you.

① **Take a long piece of string or rope** (or even a ball of yarn) and make a circle that is about six feet (2 m) across.

② **Stand in the middle of your circle with your wand** and turn clockwise, tracing the circle by pointing to it with your wand. Try to feel the energy flow from your body out to the tip of your wand and beyond. Be careful—you might see sparks if your magical potential is particularly strong. This is called "casting the circle."

③ **Place stones or flowers or even sticks around the perimeter of your circle.** Then sit in the middle of the circle and try to imagine that you've created a wall of energy around the perimeter of your circle. At this point you could recite an Energy Spell (see page 66) to help raise the energy and create positive thoughts inside your circle.

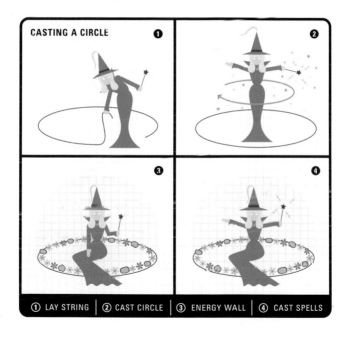

CASTING A CIRCLE ❶

❷

❸

❹

① LAY STRING | ② CAST CIRCLE | ③ ENERGY WALL | ④ CAST SPELLS

A FAMILIAR

A good witch might choose the family pet or a friendly neighborhood animal as a familiar. A bad witch will probably choose a mean-tempered animal as a familiar. More advanced witches can "morph," or take the shape of their familiar, but that requires special training and years of practice. Other common familiars include toads, owls, ravens, and dragons. Some witches like spiders, but insects can be hard to talk to.

MORPHING FAMILIARS

POOF!

NEIGHBORHOOD FAMILIARS

FLYING FAMILIARS

MEAN FAMILIARS

THE WAND

The magic wand is an essential part of the witch's equipment: it directs the flow of your magic energy. If you see sparks coming out the end of a wand, that's pure energy. Wands are usually made of wood.

1. **For a natural wand,** look for any fairly straight branch or twig that measures from about your elbow to your hand.

2. **If you're more of a city witch**, go to the hardware store and buy a wooden dowel. Decorate it with paint and glitter to infuse it with your own special magic energy.

3. **Remember**, a wand is one of your most powerful tools, so it's best not to share it with anyone.

THE HAT

The traditional witch hat has a cone shape, which symbolizes a cone of power. But these days, nobody wears formal outfits anymore (except for very special occasions). Today's fashionable witch wears a hat he or she likes—or goes bareheaded.

- **To make a traditional witch hat**, roll a cone out of black construction paper and attach a paper brim with tape. Decorate your hat to match your wand.

- **For casual days**, any hat that looks good on you will do—add decorations such as buttons or beads for extra power.

OTHER HELPFUL ITEMS

- **Herbs** (for potions and protection) Keep a pouch or bag nearby and check with a parent to see if you have some common herbs like parsley, sage, and rosemary in the cupboard. It's also a good idea to have cloves of garlic at your disposal (if you hear there's a werewolf in the neighborhood and you need to cast a protection spell) although garlic salt will do in a pinch.

- **Cauldron** (for mixing up potions) Any large pot or bucket will do, but be sure to ask your parents if you can borrow it first.
- **Amulet** (for protection and luck) Find a small stone that is meaningful to you and keep it in your pocket.
- **Cloak** (for formal occasions) Not essential but makes a dramatic fashion statement.
- **Familiar** (for company and/or inspiration) A familiar could be a real animal or it could be an imaginary creature—the trick is to pick an animal that has qualities a witch can admire (the traditional familiar is the cat because it's an independent thinker and clever, much like a witch).

It's important to remember that if you ever find yourself without any magical tools, it's the person that makes the magic, not the tools.

DON'T TRY THIS AT HOME! LEARNING TO FLY A BROOMSTICK TAKES YEARS

CTICE.

THE RULES OF WITCHERY

Modern witches DO NOT practice bad or "black" magic. If you want to be a witch, there are only two hard-and-fast rules, but you need to know them and follow them.

THE WITCH'S REDE

"As it harms none, do what you will." In other words, perform only good magic. Don't cast any spells that could hurt anyone, including yourself. This is the big one, and if you're going to practice magic, you should memorize it!

THREEFOLD LAW

"Whatever you do returns to you threefold." This rule, also known as the Rule of Three, says that whatever you do will be returned to you three times over. This doesn't necessarily mean that if you create a spell asking for the return of your favorite hat you lost on the ski slope last winter that you will suddenly get three favorite hats back! It's more of a warning to do and think good deeds and thoughts.

Remember, if you forget the Witch's Rede and the Threefold Law, and you try to cast a spell on that kid who sits next to you so that he fails his math test, you'd better look out—your next test may be a big flop!

BE CAREFUL WHAT YOU *WITCH* FOR! SPELLS CAN SURPRISE YOU!

MAGIC SYMBOLS & SPELLS

The first thing to remember about developing your magical skills (sometimes called *magickal skills*, to distinguish them from magician's magic) is that it's all about creating and directing your energy. Spell-work takes concentration and imagination. Begin by thinking about why you want to create a spell. And be really clear about what you want to achieve by casting the spell. (And don't forget your Witch's Rede and Threefold Law!)

THE MOON

Did you know that there are 13 full moons during a calendar year? It's important to know when they occur, because this is the time when magic will be strongest. Full-moon energy is used for banishing unwanted influences, protection, and divination (seeing the future). Full-moon magic can be done for seven days—three days prior to and three days after the full moon. As the moon waxes, or grows larger, that's the best time for casting spells for love, prosperity, and good health. As the moon wanes, or grows smaller, it's time to cast spells for stopping bad habits and getting rid of bad health.

WITCHES OFTEN GET TOGETHER IN GROUPS TO CELEBRATE FULL MOONS

MAGICAL SYMBOLS

Have you ever had a dream that seemed to make no sense—but you still understood what it meant? Something similar can happen with magic. You might look into a crystal ball to see the future and instead see a vision that makes no sense—like a cow and a turtle boarding an airplane. Don't be alarmed—this doesn't mean your witch powers have departed—it's probably a symbolic vision. Symbols are words or images that have meanings beyond what they seem to say. That's one of the cool things about magic—it's not always obvious.

Symbols can give you a lot of information, but you have to know what the symbols mean in order to interpret what you are seeing. The chart on the next page shows some of the traditional meanings of symbols in magic, but remember that your own special symbols are important, too.

MAGICAL SYMBOLS

1. **ROSE:** LOVE
2. **BUTTERFLY:** UNNECESSARY THINGS
3. **SEASHELL:** CREATIVITY
4. **HUMMINGBIRD:** COMMUNICATION
5. **BASKET:** GIFT
6. **CAT:** WISDOM
7. **ARROW:** NEWS
8. **SPIDER:** VERY GOOD FORTUNE
9. **HAT:** RIVAL
10. **TURTLE:** RETREAT
11. **TREE:** GOOD LUCK
12. **CLOCK:** CHANGE
13. **OWL:** WISDOM
14. **AIRPLANE:** TRAVEL
15. **COW:** MONEY
16. **WHEEL:** SEASONS, COMPLETION, ETERNITY
17. **SNAKE:** WISDOM, ETERNITY, KNOWLEDGE
18. **CROWN:** SUCCESS
19. **SPOON:** LUCK
20. **BIRD:** PSYCHIC POWERS, MOVEMENT, GOOD LUCK

DEVELOPING YOUR MAGICAL SKILLS

There are many reasons why you'd want to create a spell. Maybe you want to rid the neighborhood of a bothersome beast or maybe you hope to get a better grade on a social studies test. Your job is to figure out what you want a spell to do before trying to cast one—otherwise it could get very confusing (what if that beast ended up in your social studies class because you were thinking about both things at the same time?).

A spell is a combination of three things: saying specific words (usually a set of words that rhyme, which is more powerful than regular sentences), harnessing your personal energy, and visualizing or "seeing" the results of the spell.

HOW TO CONSTRUCT A SPELL

① **Clearly understand and define your magical goal.**
Tackle it like you would a school project—so instead of a vague goal like "being popular," think of something specific, like "make a new friend."

② **Plan your wording.** You can write out your spell until you are sure you've got it right. A spell can be two lines or fifty lines long; there's no right or wrong length. Also, there are no right or wrong words to use. Sometimes it's more fun (and easier to remember) if your spells rhyme, and you can use made-up silly words as well.

③ **Choose your magical tools.** Empower tools (stones, herbs, cords) by either holding them in your hand or pointing your wand at them. You should feel the energy flow from you into the magical tool.

④ **Decide when you want to do the spell**. Certain times are more magical than others. Check when the Witch Holidays are on your calendar. For example, while other people are waiting to see if the groundhog sees his shadow, you can be preparing your spell.

⑤ **Gather your magical tools and go to your magical space**. This can be any place where you can concentrate; it could be your closet or a corner of your backyard. Wherever it is, it should be an area big enough to allow you to make your magic circle.

⑥ **Prepare the magic circle**. First, to rid the circle of unwanted energy, take your broomstick and pretend to sweep the area. (You can really sweep if you want to—it never hurts to be clean—but use a regular broom, because your witch's broomstick might break into a thousand twigs if you use it to sweep.) Say two times:

I'm casting my circle
Just for me
Ooh-bop-a-loo-bop
Fiddle-dee-dee

• As you recite your spell, try to see or visualize your spell working.

• Wave your wand. Some witches find that moving their hands in a magical pattern works, too. Making a big figure eight in the air is one pattern, or you can wave your wand in a tight circle over your head. (Patterns can be found in any first-year course on Elementary Wand Waving at a Witch Academy—or you can make up your own.)

• Record your efforts in your Witch's Journal Write down any feelings you had while you were working your spell, and be sure to note how well it worked.

USING THE ELEMENTS—
EARTH, AIR, WATER, FIRE

In ancient times, many people thought that everything could be broken down into the four components, or elements: earth (or dirt), air, water, and fire. So when witches were first developing magic, they came up with a system in which these four elements ruled certain aspects of the spells. Knowing which elements to call on will help your spells work better.

• The earth represents our home and is the foundation of all the elements—it governs stone, tree, and knot magic.

• Air is the element of the mind—it rules spells involving travel, freedom, obtaining knowledge, discovering lost items, and uncovering lies.

• Fire is the element of change, will, and passion—it rules spells involving energy, authority, healing, and destruction of bad habits.

• Water is the element of purification and love—it rules spells involving friendship, happiness, and healing.

What does all this mean? If you use the name of the element in your spell, it helps your spell work better. For example, if you want to create a spell about getting rid of a bad habit, like biting your fingernails, you might say:

Thunderstorms and lightning bolts,
Dragons breathe out fire,
When I want to bite my nails,
I'll find my arm feels tired.

ENERGY SPELL

Here's a spell you might use for raising and sending energy—or creating positive thoughts for any purpose. Suppose you've got a baseball game tomorrow—this would be the time to use the Energy Spell. Or maybe everyone in your house has come down with the purple-spotted yellow-cheeked flu and you don't want to get sick. Think positive and use the Energy Spell.

Take up your position in your magic circle. Make sure you have your wand in your hand so you can draw a figure eight over your head as you recite the following words:

Air breathe and air blow
Make the mill of magic grow

When cats and dogs come out to play
Let the magic rise today

Lions, and tigers, and bears, oh my,
Put the magic 'round my eye

With unicorns and dragons near
Put the magic in my ear

Because the wind is from the south
Put the magic in my mouth

As the rain begins to start
Put the magic in my heart

When snails run and chickens sing
I'm not afraid of anything

Repeat this spell whenever you need a little boost in your energy, your courage, or your positive thinking.

PUT A LITTLE MAGIC
IN YOUR LIFE

If you are a witch, or training to become one, you'll want to do a bit of magic every day. You might do a good deed, like helping find something that is lost, or maybe you'll just try to have a little fun and bring happy energy to a friend's birthday party. Here are some ways to work everyday magic.

YOUR POWER HAND: One of your hands is your power hand. How do you tell which one? It's the hand you hold your wand in—if you're right-handed it might be your right hand, but maybe not. Shift your wand from hand to hand and see where it feels best—that's your power hand.

STONE MAGIC

You probably didn't realize it, but regular stones—like the stones in your driveway, on the beach, or in a stream—can help you make magic.

The first thing you have to do when working with stones is to figure out their energy—is it a high-energy or a low-energy stone? Take a stone that you like (sometimes you don't even know why you like a particular stone but you just find yourself picking it up anyway) and then hold it in your hand. Sit quietly and feel the stone in your hand and think about all the properties of that stone—is it rounded and smooth or does it have some jagged edges? Is it a color you like? Does it feel warm or cold? Then clear your mind of all thoughts and just hold the stone. You might be able to feel tingling or vibrations in your hand. Are they fast or slow? As a rule of thumb, the brighter the color of the stone, the higher the energy or the faster the vibration (for example, a red stone would have a faster vibration than a black one). Do this with every stone you want to use for your magic and sort them into two piles. For some spells you want a high-energy stone and for others a low-energy stone.

WHAT COLOR IS MY STONE?

Different powers are associated with different colors:

WHITE: ⚪	PEACE, TRANQUILITY
GREEN: 🟢	LOVE, MONEY
RED: 🔴	PASSION, ARGUMENTS
ORANGE 🟠	LUCK
YELLOW: ⚪	WISDOM, LESSONS
BROWN: 🟤	OBJECTS, POSSESSIONS, GIFTS
BLACK: ⚫	NEGATIVITY

CREATE A GOOD-LUCK CHARM

Take a small, high-vibration stone and sit in your magic circle, holding the stone in your power hand. Sit quietly and stare at the stone. When you are feeling relaxed (not so relaxed that you fall asleep!) start to recite your spell. There's no right or wrong spell, although you'll need to get across the idea that you want the stone to protect you. You might try something like the following, but don't be afraid to make up your own spells; they should mean something to you—so if you're a funny person, make them funny!

Higgety, piggety, turkey trot,
Sometimes a good stone is hard to spot
But I've got one that'll make my day
Each time I touch it, protect my way

(continued on next page)

CREATE A GOOD-LUCK CHARM

(continued from previous page)

Dog's breath, cat's knees
I want a stone to help me please,
If I'm in trouble, or begin to see double,
Please surround me in an invisible bubble

Carry your stone with you at all times as a good-luck amulet. If your spell worked, the stone will absorb your vibrations and then release its energies to form a kind of protective shield around you.

SEE THE FUTURE

Magic stones can help you find answers to some burning questions—like, "Does the girl who sits next to me in social studies like me?" or, "Will I get a good grade on my math test?"

Select three stones from your stone collection. One should be a bright color/high-energy stone: this is your **yes** stone. Another should be a dark color/low-energy stone: this is your **no** stone. The third should be of an entirely different color from the other two and of a medium energy: this is your **indicator** stone. Together, these are your **divining stones**.

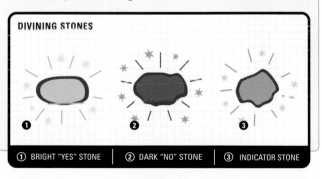

DIVINING STONES

① BRIGHT "YES" STONE ② DARK "NO" STONE ③ INDICATOR STONE

SEE THE FUTURE

① Sit in your magic circle with your three stones in your hand.

② As you think of your question, throw the stones on the ground the same way you would roll dice. It's a lot more fun if you can make up a spell that contains your question and then say it out loud. Examples might be:

Levitator mercurator,
Take me up the escalator,
When I get up to the top,
Will I find what I want when I shop?
Or
Heckle, jeckle,
Froggety frog,
Tomorrow will I get a dog?

③ If the "yes" stone ends up closest to the indicator stone, the answer is yes. If the "no" ends up closest to the indicator stone, the answer is no.

④ If they both seem to be an equal distance away from the indicator stone, there is no answer. Try phrasing the question differently.

Your divining stones should be kept separate from your other stones, in their own little pouch (a plastic baggie would do nicely), and they should be used for no other purposes.

MIRROR MAGIC

You may not have realized it but mirrors can be a source of magic. Not regular mirrors, of course, only those with magical powers from the full moon. You can create a magic mirror in which to see visions of the future or even to find things that are lost.

CHARGE YOUR MIRROR WITH THE POWER OF THE MOON

First, find a round mirror of any size—a compact mirror or a hand mirror will do nicely. But remember that this is going to be a special mirror, so don't choose a mirror someone in your house uses every day. Next, wash the mirror's face carefully with clean water. When it's dry, cover its face with a dark cloth and put it where it won't be touched until the next full moon.

When the full moon rises (this is often early in the evening) you can either go outside with your mirror or hold your mirror up to the window so that the moon is reflected in it. This is called charging your mirror or giving it the moon's energy. Then say:

Mirror, mirror, one, two, three
Mirror, mirror, do you see
When you look into the moon
Feel the power come in you soon

Cover your mirror with the dark cloth when you're not using it. Remember, this is your magic mirror and is only supposed to be used for divination, *not* for checking whether you have toothpaste on your cheek or if your hair is combed. Be sure to recharge your mirror—show it to the full moon—at least three times a year.

KNOT MAGIC

Knot magic is a very old form of magic.

Knot magic is generally performed with colored string or rope. In a pinch, even thread will do. Use natural fibers like wool or cotton if possible, and avoid stiff, rough, slippery, or plastic cords.

SIMPLE KNOT SPELL

Use this spell to wish for anything you might need, such as a good grade on your next English test or a new pair of sneakers.

1. Take about one foot (30 cm) of any color string or rope that you like.

2. Think really hard about what you need (and remember, only one thing at a time!) while holding the string tight in your hands.

③ While you're thinking recite a little spell like "Crater, traitor, midnight raider, make me a human calculator" (to help with a math test wish). Remember to make up your spell ahead of time.

④ While you're concentrating really hard, tie a knot in the string.

⑤ Pull the ends of the string tight—this releases the energy to go and do your bidding.

The knotted string is a reminder of your wish, so keep the string with you (maybe in your pocket) or somewhere safe in your room. If you wished for something that might take a while to come true, like a new friend or tickets to the Olympics, you might want to put the string in a box and bury the box in the backyard to make sure it won't ever be found or come unknotted.

If you wish to undo or reverse the spell, untie the knot, but be aware that you can't always reverse a spell.

BINDING

Suppose a friend wants to borrow something of yours and you're worried that you won't get it back? This spell will help make sure it's returned. Let's say your friend wants to borrow your favorite CD, and you're not sure you want to lend it to her because she never returns the stuff she borrows. This spell might help.

Take the CD she wants to borrow and a length of string—use either orange, a color associated with legal matters (like a contract), or black, which has binding properties—and literally tie the CD to yourself.

① Wrap one end of the string around the CD and make a knot, then take the other end and tie it around your wrist or your hand.

② Keep the CD tied to you for a couple of minutes, all the while imagining it coming back into your CD collection.

③ Then—this is important—cut the string from around the CD but do not cut the knot. Then cut the string from around your wrist or hand, again making sure not to cut through the knot.

④ Put the string in a safe place until the CD returns.

This will work with any object. Obviously if it's a large object you can't wrap the string around the whole thing, so just tie part of it to you. You should, however, picture the whole object so that if someone borrows your bike and you bind yourself to the handle bars or the front wheel you don't just get the front tire back!

Binding can be very powerful magic, so make sure you don't bind yourself to objects that you might want to give away as presents at some point. That present just might bounce back, whether you want it to or not!

CHAPTER FIVE

A WITCH'S RESOURCES

Glinda, Kiki, Samantha, _____. This space is for your name. Go ahead and write it in! Now you are in the company of some famous good witches. Remember, people spend years perfecting their witchy ways—but don't dismay. By reading this book you have been introduced to the wonderful world of witches and some of the basic spells. Who knows? Maybe your magical potential will surprise you!

FURTHER READING AND VIEWING

BOOKS

Bed-Knobs and Broomsticks, by Mary Norton (1943)

Harry Potter and the Goblet of Fire, by J. K. Rowling (2000)

Harry Potter and the Prisoner of Azkaban, by J. K. Rowling (2000)

Harry Potter and the Secret Chamber, by J. K. Rowling (1999)

Harry Potter and the Sorcerer's Stone, by J. K. Rowling (1997)

Macbeth, by William Shakespeare

The Lion, the Witch and the Wardrobe, by C. S. Lewis (1950)

The Little Witch's Big Night, by Deborah Hautzig (1984)

The Witches, by Roald Dahl (1983)

MOVIES

Escape to Witch Mountain, directed by John Hough (1975)

Harry Potter and the Sorcerer's Stone, directed by Chris Columbus (2001)

Hocus Pocus, directed by Kenny Ortega (1993)

I Married a Witch, directed by Rene Clair (1942)

Kiki's Delivery Service, directed by Hayao Miyazaki (1989)

Return to Witch Mountain, directed by John Hough (1978)

The Witches, directed by Nicolas Roeg (1990)

The Wizard of Oz, directed by Victor Fleming and King Vidor (1939)

Wonderworks: The Chronicles of Narnia – The Lion, the Witch and the Wardrobe, directed by Marilyn Fox (1988)

TELEVISION SHOWS

Charmed

Sabrina, the Teenage Witch

GLOSSARY

Amulet: A natural object like a stone or a feather that you have charged with your magical energy. Often worn around the neck to protect you from bad things.

Besom (BEE-sum): The witch's broomstick.

Charging: Same as enchanting and empowering. Sending your own personal energy into an object, like an herb or a stone, that will then help you with your magic.

Circle: The space you create with your wand to do your spell work.

Familiar: A witch's coworker that is of a non-human form. Many times a cat, but other popular familiars are toads, owls, and dogs.

Threefold Law: Basically states that the energy released by an individual, either positive or negative, will return to the sender three times over.

Visualization: Seeing in your mind what you wish for. This is used in spell work. Wishing is not enough; you have to visualize it.

Wand: A tool used to direct energy. You hold your wand in your dominant, or power, hand.

Witch's Journal: The spell book or journal used by a witch to record his or her thoughts. Some witch's call the journal a Book of Shadows, because an un-worked spell is a mere shadow, not taking form until performed by a witch.

Witch's Rede: "As it harms none, do what you will." The rede prohibits witches from harming any other living thing or violating anyone's free will.

WITCH'S JOURNAL

WITCH HOLIDAYS AND FULL MOONS THIS YEAR:

MAGICAL DREAMS:

MY FAVORITE SPELLS:

❶

WHEN I USED IT:

HOW IT WORKED:

❷

WHEN I USED IT:

HOW IT WORKED:

PERSONAL SYMBOLS:

WITCH IDENTIFICATION

UNITED ORGANIZATION OF
PERSONS OF EXTRAORDINARY
MAGICAL POTENTIAL
(U.O.P.E.M.P.)

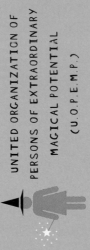

The bearer of this card has read and understood *The Witch's Handbook* and is hereby licensed to practice witchery in countries throughout the world. Possession of this ID certifies that the bearer has extraordinary magical potential, can cast spells, is in possession of a wand, and might have a fondness for black, pointy hats. The undersigned also pledges to use magical abilities for good rather than evil. Please give the bearer unlimited access to any airspace you might control.